BRUCE McCALL

Marveltown

FARRAR, STRAUS AND GIROUX
NEW YORK

JP McCall

To Polly and Amanda

Copyright © 2008 by Bruce McCall
All rights reserved
Distributed in Canada by Douglas & McIntyre Ltd.
Color separations by Embassy Graphics
Printed and bound in China by South China Printing Co. Ltd.
Designed by Jay Colvin
First edition, 2008
1 3 5 7 9 10 8 6 4 2

www.fsgkidsbooks.com

Library of Congress Cataloging-in-Publication Data
McCall, Bruce.
    Marveltown / Bruce McCall.— 1st ed.
        p.   cm.
    Summary: Marveltown's adults are outstanding inventors, but when their best
engineers create giant but stupid robots that threaten the town, it is the children's
outrageous creations that save the day.
    ISBN-13: 978-0-374-39925-2
    ISBN-10: 0-374-39925-5
    [1. Inventions—Fiction.   2. Robots—Fiction.   3. Science fiction.]   I. Title.

PZ7.M12288Mar 2008
[E]—dc22   2006038250

Sky-skiing! The very idea would buckle the knees of most people. Not us Marveltown kids! In fact, we *invented* sky-skiing.

Who couldn't spare five minutes for a car wash? Marveltowners couldn't. That's how we kids learned that faster was always better.

And bigger was better, too. Take Flipover Farm—a huge disk of farmland that turned over every December to reveal a winter playground. Come spring, it turned over again and the farmland was back.

The incredible new Skyway was held up by *invisible ion rays*. No one had tried such a project before, so at first, construction was slow and costly. Couldn't all those big Marveltown brains find a better way?

From its floating freeway to its mechanical-animal zoo, Marveltown inspired us kids to daydream about the great things we'd invent someday.

And we'd jump at any chance to try making our daydreams come true.

Every Saturday, the grownups threw open the doors to the Invent-o-Drome and gave Marveltown kids free rein.

We'd scour the Storage Center for supplies. It was an inventor's paradise.

The Rocket Chair was my idea. I'd always been late for school; now
I could shoot from backyard to schoolyard in six seconds flat!

That's Babette launching her invention—the world's largest flying model.
Big as a barn, but light as a feather.

The strange thing in the distance is the Human Machine Gun, my pal Kurt's idea. It could fire sixty kids a minute into the air—at least in theory. Kurt never did find sixty volunteers.

What could the teacher do? "The dog ate my homework" was true! Felix, the inventor of the Homework Grinder, charged a nickel a chew.

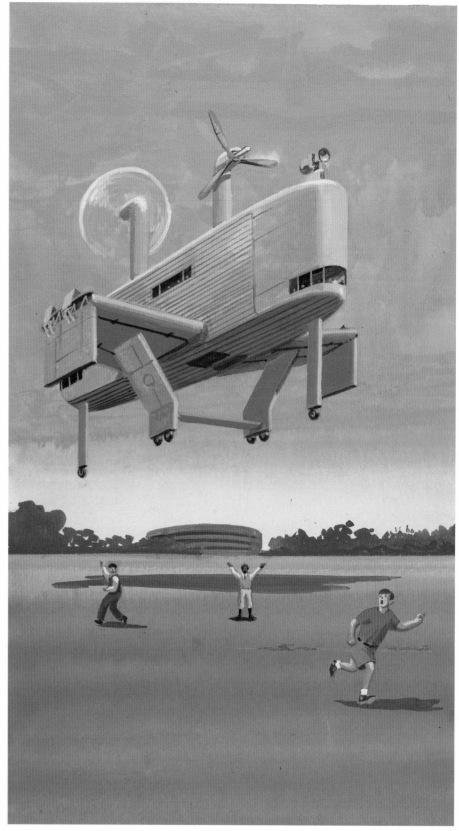

Willard's mom was so dazed by his Hypno-Goggles, he could get away with anything. Floyd's reversible Aero-Whale could change direction in midair.

Fenwick invented the radio-controlled Ripple Rug especially for tripping up school bullies.

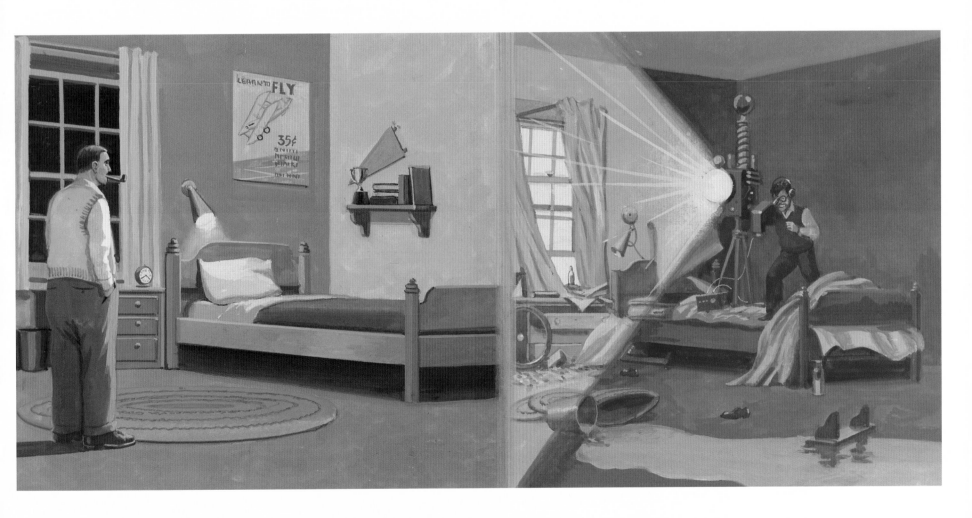

Eli's bedroom hologram was diabolical: Dad saw spick-and-span perfection, when the reality was a place that you wouldn't want to live in.

While Marveltown kids were inventing away, so were our parents—and soon they cracked their Skyway problem: the airborne road could be speedily built using giant electrohydraulic robots!

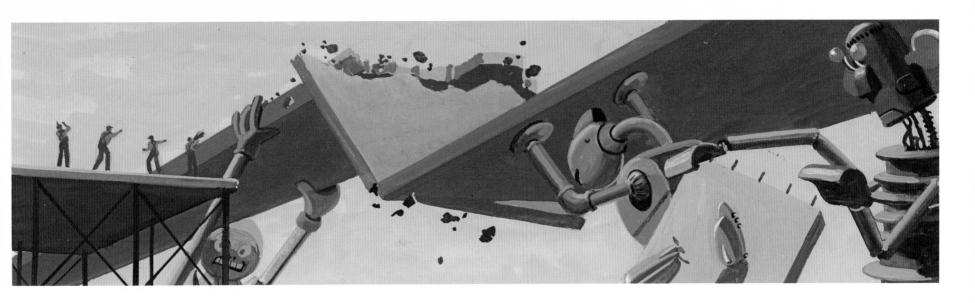

The first robots were, frankly, duds—stumbling and fumbling, knocking things down, just making a shambles of whatever they touched.

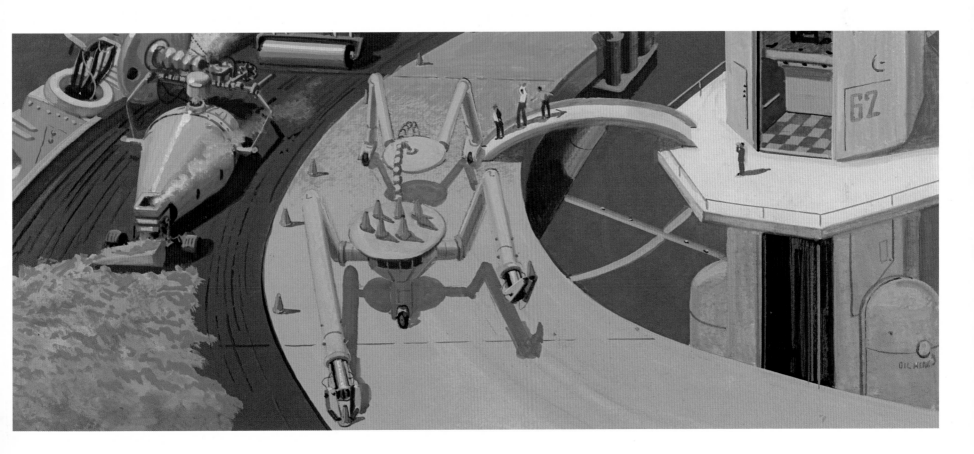

But the fixes came quick, and eventually the adults came up with robots for every chore: lifting, welding, paving, even going for coffee. The Skyway project was rolling at last!

Until one quiet midnight . . . when deep inside Robot Central Command, a curious mouse chewed through a cable. *Zap!* The whole system short-circuited. And in the chaos that followed, the same mangled message went out to every robot: YOUR ROCKS JOB: FJ CRUSH FTEY9 MARVELTXWN!!

Dawn's first light revealed an army of colossal mechanical morons marching toward Marveltown.

As the menacing monsters approached, Marveltowners panicked: "Run for your lives! We're all doomed!"

Not so fast, folks! The grownups might flee—but the kids were already in action. Felix's Homework Grinder made a perfect guard dog. My Rocket Chair bowled over more than one mighty electrohydraulic dunce.

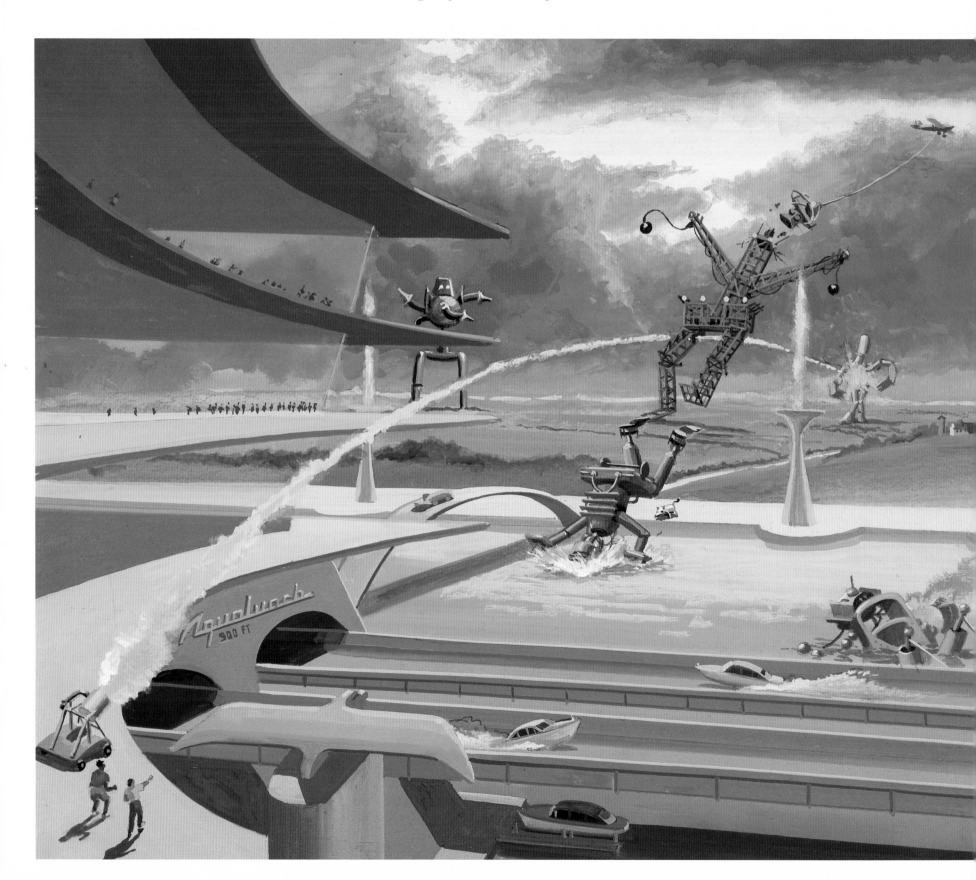

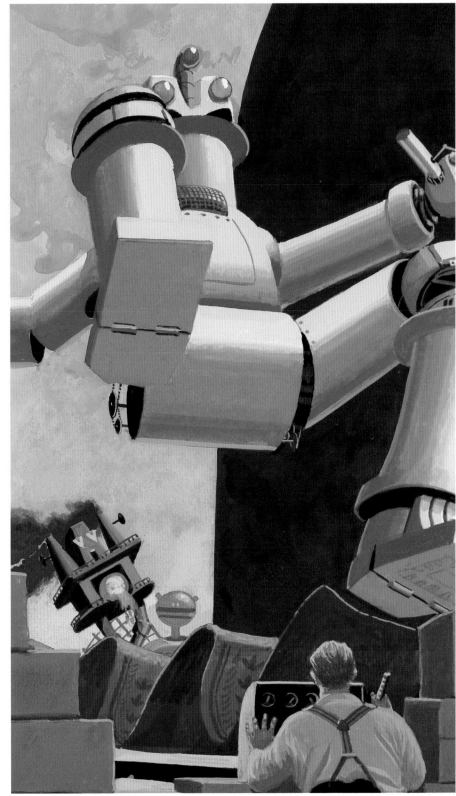

Willard beamed those Hypno-Goggles of his at the robots and sent them reeling. Fenwick's Ripple Rug became a booby trap for every slow-footed goliath.

The kids of Marveltown taught those tin-suited knuckleheads a lesson.

Everywhere, super-sly kid power was clobbering brute robot power!

The grownups slowly crawled out from their hideaways. What they saw was that we kids—the kids of Marveltown—had earned a place in history.

The attack doomed the Skyway: nobody trusted robots anymore, and no robots meant no Skyway.

But we kids had proven ourselves. And as inventors, we were just getting started.
Who knew what big brainstorms were next?